You make my day!

Stamp

Red and Slim

One Hot Day

By Stamp

Illustrated by Utopia Joe

When Red and Slim set out to find a drink on a hot day, they find one thing more, that friends need each other.

Requests for permission to make copies or any part of the work
should be mailed to the following address:
Permission Department, Syllabets Press, LLC.,
2692 Madison Rd. Suite N1-377, Cincinnati, OH 45208

www.syllabets.com

Library of Congress Cataloging-in-Publication Data
Stamp, Jeffrey A., 1960-
Red & Slim One Hot Day / Jeffrey A. Stamp
Summary: When Red and Slim set out to find a drink on a hot day, they find
one thing more, that friends need each other.
[1. Friendship – Fiction. 2. Adventure – Fiction. 3. Self-esteem – Fiction. 4. Problem Solving – Fiction]
ISBN-13: 978-0-9794543-0-1   ISBN-10: 0-9794543-0-1

Syllabets I Can Read It! Series
Red & Slim "One Hot Day"
First edition
10 9 8 7 6 5 4 3 2 1

Written by Jeffrey A. Stamp, PhD
Illustrated by Joe Boher and was rendered in ink on illustration board (www.utopiajoe.com)
Concept pencil illustrations by Nick Hermes
Cover design and layout by AuthorSupport.com
Printed in the U.S.A. by Forum Communications, Fargo, ND
Bound by Muscle Bound Bindery, Minneapolis, MN

To JJ and Alyssa
You make my day.

It was a hot day.

Slim the cat, and Red the dog did
not want to go out.

But the man made them.

Slim was sad.

Red was sad.

It was so hot.

The pot they drink from was dry as dirt.

Slim took his cup, "This is dry.
Can you find a drink?"

Red did not run. It was too hot.

Slim first made a hat to fit on top of his head.

His new hat made Red grin.

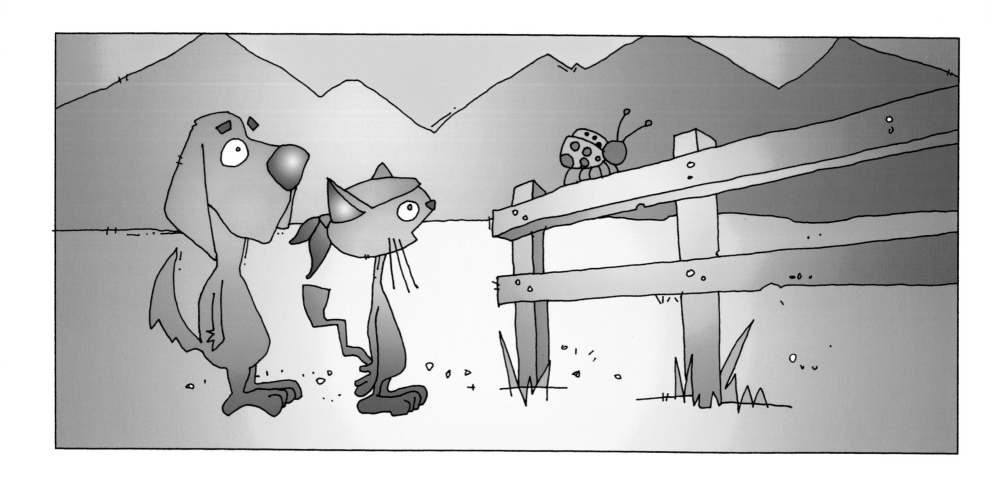

Slim saw a bug. "Do you know where we can find a drink?"

The bug gave a shrug and flew
off in the hot wind.

"Wow," said Red, "that bug was not much fun."

"I know what to do. Stay with me."

So they went down the road.

Soon Slim saw an old bus.

"Do you know where we can find
a drink?"

The old bus made no sound.
He was not in the mood to talk.

He had no tires.

Red said to Slim, "Where does the man get a drink?"

Slim had a grin. "I know, in the house."

"But how do we get in?" cried Red.

Slim went to the back of the house.

He saw a chance.

"Do you think you can make it, Red?"

"Sure," and Slim put out his paw
to help Red up.

Then Slim had to hop up on his own.

Red gave him a pat on the back.

Slim made his way up the stairs.

Red could not wait to see what was next.

Then Slim went in the door.

He made a run for the tub.

Slim made a big splash.

Red made a big splash.

They had lots to drink.

Red gave Slim a hug.

"You are my best friend."

"You are all wet."

The End
For now...

Our tale is done. But there is more to ask.

Did you know all books can live in your mind?

Do Red and Slim?

Think on what you just read. What were Red and Slim in search of? Can you see it in your mind? Can you name it?

See www.syllabets.com to see how well you know the whole tale.

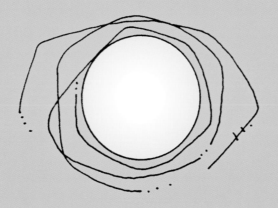